*STORY AND PICTURES BY IVAN GANTSCHEV*

# JOURNEY OF THE STORKS

*NEUGEBAUER PRESS USA*

For a long time the stork's nest in the village has been empty.
The people of this little northern town would love to have a
stork family of their own. Often they wave to the storks as they
fly past the church steeple and over the town.
"Stay here!" they call. But the storks fly on to other villages,
and the people look sadly at the empty nest.

Then one day a large and beautiful stork lands in the nest.
Surprised and happy, the townspeople look up at the chimney.
The pigeon, too, looks across curiously from a nearby roof.
But here comes another stork! At long last, a stork couple has found
its home here. The two of them make it cozy. Here and there they pull
the nest together and cushion it. Soon the nest looks much softer
and warmer.

How happy the villagers are when the stork
and his wife have a child!
"Shall we call the little stork Jacob?" they ask each other.
Everyone watches how little Jacob learns to fly.
He does quite well. His wings seem to know
just what to do. Jacob is never afraid, for his
mother is always nearby.

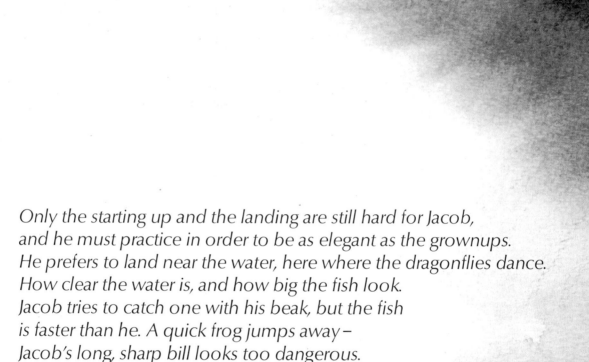

Only the starting up and the landing are still hard for Jacob,
and he must practice in order to be as elegant as the grownups.
He prefers to land near the water, here where the dragonflies dance.
How clear the water is, and how big the fish look.
Jacob tries to catch one with his beak, but the fish
is faster than he. A quick frog jumps away –
Jacob's long, sharp bill looks too dangerous.

One cool autumn morning the storks meet at the riverbank. Like the others, Jacob feels restless and excited. "Today we begin flying towards the South, where it is warmer than here," his mother says. "Now you are big enough for your first journey."

*As they set off through the gray morning sky, little Jacob flies along behind his mother.*

As they fly along together Jacob is full of questions.
"Are those toy cows and toy houses?" he asks his mother.
"No, they are real," she tells him, "but we are flying
much higher than usual so that we can fly above the
tallest mountains. That's why everything looks so tiny."
"But those blue eyes looking up at us aren't tiny."
"That's because they are actually deep
mountain lakes, Jacob."

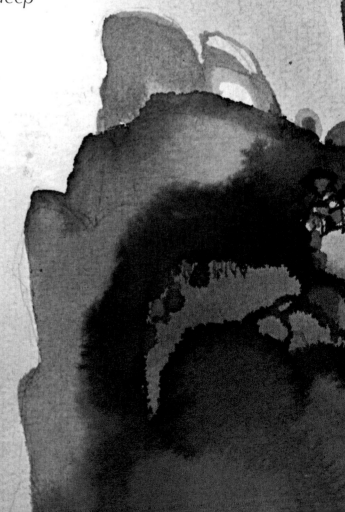

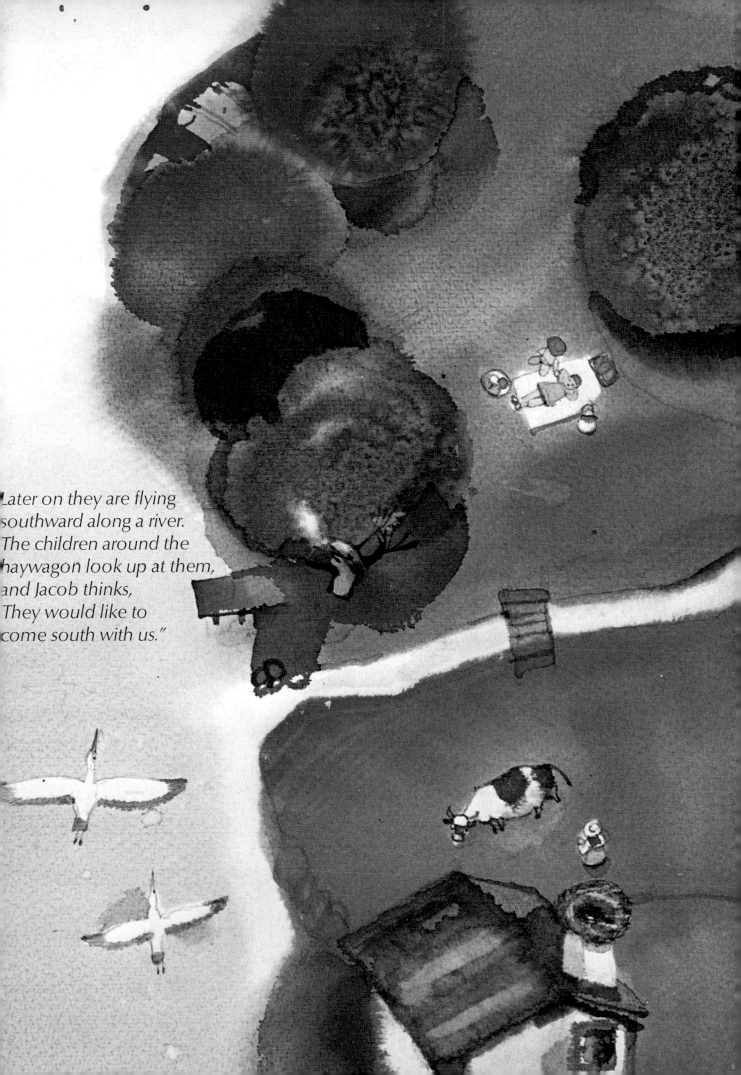

"Later on they are flying southward along a river. The children around the haywagon look up at them, and Jacob thinks, They would like to come south with us."

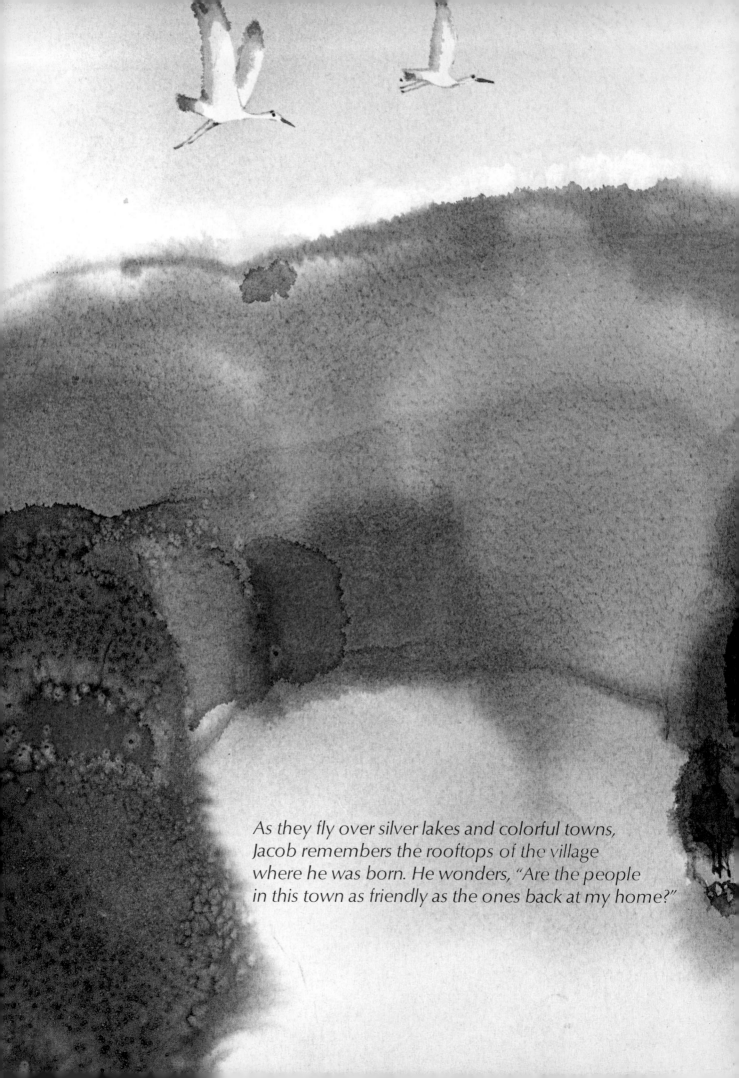

As they fly over silver lakes and colorful towns,
Jacob remembers the rooftops of the village
where he was born. He wonders, "Are the people
in this town as friendly as the ones back at my home?"

The closer they get to the sea,
the wider the rivers become.
More and more often, Jacob asks his mother,
"When do we come to the South?"
"Not yet, little one," she answers.
"Look! The children are waving to us,"
he says to his mother. "They are inviting us –
let's stay here! Why don't we?"

"We have to go on," his mother says.
"There is still a long way to go."

This is the sea. It is so large that Jacob cannot tell where it begins
or where it will end. He is a little worried, but fortunately,
all the other storks are with him. And there, far below them
is a ship. It is going the same direction they are, but the storks
are so much faster that they soon leave the ship far behind.

And what is this?
It almost looks like a birthday cake, but bigger,
and more colorful, and much more beautiful.
"This is a palace," his mother says.
"A great prince lives here."
"Is this the South? Are we staying here?"
asks Jacob again.
"We must keep going," she answers.

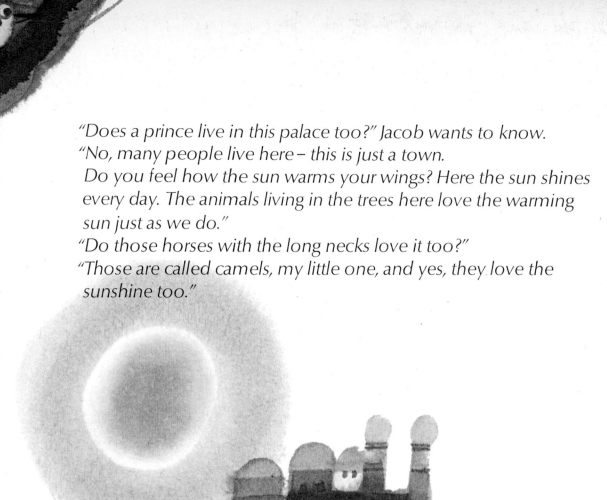

"Does a prince live in this palace too?" Jacob wants to know.
"No, many people live here – this is just a town.
Do you feel how the sun warms your wings? Here the sun shines
every day. The animals living in the trees here love the warming
sun just as we do."
"Do those horses with the long necks love it too?"
"Those are called camels, my little one, and yes, they love the
sunshine too."

"We are here at last!"
After many, many days, the storks have reached their destination.
What a journey!
The mother cleans her feathers and clicks her bill as a greeting.
"These two children from the town have been waiting for us. We will live
in this tree until it is warmer again at our home in the North."
Jacob is very happy. He is glad to be warm, he is glad to see the
friendly children from the town, and he is very glad to be at the end
of his long, long journey.

In the North, it is wintertime now, and Jacob's nest has completely disappeared under a cold covering of snow. But the townspeople have not forgotten their little stork. They are all hoping that he will return, since they know he will bring back the flowers and blossoms of spring, and then the warm summer sun. They all have the same wish: "Jacob, come back again soon!"

May 1995